A Week at Grandma Ruth's

written and photographed
by
Mia Coulton

For my Grandma Ruth, Mima

Danny's Big Adventure #3

A Week at Grandma Ruth's

Published by:
MaryRuth Books, Inc.
18660 Ravenna Road
Chagrin Falls, OH 44023

www.maryruthbooks.com

Editor: Heidi Maleka

Library of Congress Control Number: 2008932778
ISBN 978-1-933624-26-6

Printed in the United States of America
10 9 8 7 6 5 4 3 2

SPC/0310/16461

Contents

Grandma Ruth   4

The Woods   16

Frank   22

Maple Festival   30

Going Home   38

Grandma Ruth

One warm spring day, Danny and Dad went to visit Grandma Ruth. They were going to stay for one week!

Grandma Ruth lived in a white house out in the country, far away from Danny and Dad's house. She was Dad's mom, but he called her Grandma Ruth, too.

Danny loved the white house.

He loved the kitchen. It was big with a black and white checked floor. And it always smelled like fresh baked cookies and cakes.

But what Danny loved most about the white house was that Grandma Ruth lived there.

Grandma Ruth wore funny shoes. They were pink with little bees.

She wore blue jeans unless it was a special day, like Sunday.

That is when she would wear her pretty pink dress that matched her pink shoes with little bees.

Grandma Ruth was always glad to see Danny.

"Oh my stars," she said, "my, how you've grown."

She patted Danny on the head and said, "I just baked something special for you. Come on in and have a look."

And that is just what he did.

Dad went back to the car to get the luggage.

Danny followed him.
Dad brought in all the luggage.

Danny brought in his bed and Bee, too.

Danny put his bed in the corner of the kitchen. It was warm in the kitchen at night.

He put Bee in his bed.

He wanted to make sure Bee

was in his bed when it was

time to go to sleep.

He got his bowl out of his luggage and went to put it on the bone mat but saw that Grandma Ruth already had a bowl for him.

He got his leash out of his luggage and started to look around the kitchen for a place to hang it.

Grandma Ruth saw him and said, "No need for a leash here, Danny Boy, you're a country dog this week."

"A country dog," Danny wondered, "what exactly is a country dog?"

"Let's take a look out back," said Grandma Ruth. She took off her pink shoes with the little bees and put on her muck boots. They were blue with green polka dots and good for mucking around in the mud.

Dad put on his muck boots, too.

They all walked around for a bit.

It was very muddy way out back.

"Can you help me clean this place

up?" asked Grandma Ruth.

"Sure," said Dad, "I love to work

outdoors." Danny was bored with

all the work talk. So he went to

look for an adventure.

The Woods

Grandma Ruth had woods behind her house. That was the best place to explore and find an adventure.

Danny loved to walk in the woods. He loved to hear the *crunch, crunch* as he walked down the path in the woods. He loved to sniff under logs and look down big holes.

Suddenly, Danny saw something yellow run right past him. Then he saw it again.

Now it was running toward him.

It was running very fast.

It stopped and looked at Danny.

It was a dog! Danny thought he

was looking into a mirror because

the dog looked just like him.

Danny was so surprised!
He turned and ran all the way
back to the house without
looking back. He plopped down
on the back stoop with his fat,
pink tongue hanging out.

Dad and Grandma Ruth were in the kitchen making work plans. Dad heard Danny.

He got up from the table and came to the back door to see what was going on.

"What's wrong Danny? You look like you've seen a ghost," said Dad.

Frank

Grandma Ruth came to the back door and said, "I have a surprise for you boys."

She put her two fingers in her mouth and gave a loud whistle.

A dog came running out of the woods. It was the same dog Danny had seen in the woods.

"Meet Frank," she said.

Dad looked at Danny and said,

"*Frank*???"

Grandma Ruth said, "Frank's my new dog. Farmer Frank sold his farm and was moving to the city. He couldn't take his pup with him so he gave him to me. I named him after Farmer Frank. I thought it would be fun for Danny to have a pal when he comes to visit. And, besides, it gets lonely around here."

Danny wondered if he was named after anyone.

Danny, Dad and Frank became
fast friends.

Every morning, Danny would
wake up to find Frank sleeping
next to him. Frank had moved
his bed to the kitchen to
be close to Danny.

Danny and Frank would first eat
their breakfast, then go for a long
walk in the woods with Dad.

Just the three of them,

best friends forever.

Dad spent most of his time working outdoors.

He liked to drive big machines that could dig and move dirt. Frank liked to ride along, too.

It was great fun.

Danny liked to stay inside with Grandma Ruth because she liked to cook and bake. When she was cooking, something always seemed to drop on the floor for Danny to clean up.

It was great fun.

Maple Festival

It was Maple Festival time.

Every year, Dad, Danny and

Grandma Ruth would pile into the

car and go to the Maple Festival

to buy some fresh maple syrup.

Today it was raining. Not a nice day for the Maple Festival. Grandma Ruth didn't want to go. Dad didn't want to go. Danny didn't want to go.

Frank wanted to go. He had never been to the Maple Festival.

So Dad said, "Okay, Frank, you and I will go but just for a little bit. We need some fresh maple syrup for our pancakes."

When they got to the festival,

Dad said, "It's raining cats and

dogs! I want to go home!"

Frank did not want to go home.

He wanted to go on the rides.

Dad and Frank went to look

for the rides.

Frank saw the rides.

He got scared.

Dad said, "Frank, you're too short to go on the rides."

"Phew," sighed Frank.

Dad smelled some french fries.

He said, "Let's go get some fries

and then go home."

And that is just what they did.

Grandma Ruth and Danny were waiting outside for Dad and Frank to return from the Maple Festival. They had made some pancakes and couldn't wait to pour some fresh maple syrup on top.

"Hand over the maple syrup," said Grandma Ruth.

Dad looked at Frank.
Frank looked at Dad.

"Oops," said Dad, "we forgot the maple syrup!"

Going Home

The next morning, Danny woke up to see all the luggage packed. The week was over, and it was time to go home.

Danny wanted to stay and play with Frank. But he also wanted to go home and rest.

Dad put all the luggage into the car.

Danny put his bed and Bee into the car.

Grandma Ruth had made a picnic lunch for the long trip home. She put the basket into the backseat of the car with Danny. Danny couldn't wait to see what she had made for lunch. He took a look. He saw two sandwiches and a big bag of cookies with a note stuck on top.

Dear Danny,

Thank you so much for coming to visit me.

It was great fun.

I think Frank had an awesome time.

We must do it again soon.

Look after Dad for me and make sure he

drives carefully.

I love you "oodles."

xoxoxoxox

Grandma Ruth